Samuel French Acting Edition

I Bring You Flowers

by William Lang

I BRING YOU FLOWERS

A One-Act Play

For One Woman and One Man
and an Extra

CHARACTERS

YOUNG WOMAN   .   .   .   An attractive and appealing type

YOUNG MAN .   .   .   .   . A kind and understanding person

NURSE

TIME: The present.

PLACE: A patio-type public garden.

PRODUCTION NOTES

PROPERTIES

A representational set is all that is needed. A bench and a few real or artificial plants and flowers will indicate an outdoor patio. The young woman comes on stage pushing a baby carriage.

COSTUMES

The man and woman wear any type of fashionable modern clothes. The nurse is in a uniform, if her part is included in the production.

I BRING YOU FLOWERS

SCENE: A patio with potted flowers and shrubs nearby to indicate a part of a public patio-type garden. There is a bench in the center. It is a pleasant morning, perhaps in early summer.

AT RISE OF CURTAIN: A young woman, fashionably dressed and pushing a baby carriage, enters. She pushes the carriage to one side of the bench and sits down. She stares off into space lost in her own thoughts. After a moment or two, a young man, dressed in light weight summer clothes and carrying a newspaper under his arm, enters. He sits down beside the woman and begins reading the newspaper. It would appear that two strangers had come to this flower garden and this bench to enjoy the morning.

FAYE
It's a lovely day for flowers, isn't it?

JIM
[Looking up, turning to her, and smiling] Yes, it is.

FAYE
Do you mind if I ask you a question?

JIM
No. Not at all.

FAYE
If all the flowers in the world were stretched end to end, how long would they be?

5

                              JIM
To the moon and back.

                              FAYE
[With exaggeration]
You're kidding!

                              JIM
[With exaggeration while raising his hand in the scout salute]
Scouts honor!

                              FAYE
If all the flowers in the world were put in one big flower pot,
how high would that be?

                              JIM
Four times the height of the Empire State Building.

                              FAYE
[With exaggeration]
You're kidding!

                              JIM
[With exaggeration while raising his hand in the scout salute.]
Scouts honor!

                              FAYE
[Enjoying their game]
If all the flowers in the world were one color, what color
would that be?

                              JIM
White

                              FAYE
[With exaggeration]
You're kidding!

                              JIM
[With exaggeration while raising his hand in the scout salute.]
Scouts honor!

FAYE

If all the flowers in the world were each given, one by one, to a
little child to hold and smell . . .

JIM

[He stands and walks a few steps away. His line cuts off
FAYE's last speech. With seriousness]
No, Faye. No.

FAYE

I said if all the flowers in the world were each given to a little
child . . .

JIM

[Interrupting her again]
Faye, ask something else.

FAYE

I want to know the answer to that question.

JIM

There is no answer to that question. It disappeared.

FAYE

It didn't!

JIM

It did.

FAYE

Are you sure?

JIM

Yes, I'm sure.
[JIM goes and sits again. FAYE stares off into space and JIM
reads the paper. After a moment, he turns to her.]
Would you like to read a part of the paper?

FAYE

No, thank you. I think I'll enjoy the flowers.

                    FAYE
[Cont'd. after a long pause]
What time is it?

                    JIM
[Looking at his watch.]
Ten to ten.

                    FAYE
Time is so deceiving, I could stay here forever.

                    JIM
Ask me another question.

                    FAYE
[With enthusiasm]
How many chinamen are there in Honolulu?

                    JIM
[With enthusiasm]
Half a million and they're all waiters at Wo Fats.

                    FAYE
[With exaggeration]
You're kidding!

                    JIM
[With exaggeration while raising his hand in the scout salute.]
Scouts honor. [He stands and as he acts out the following
scene he speaks in the Hawaiian-pidgin accent common in
Hawaii. He extends his hand to FAYE and she stands. They
begin to act out an incident in a Chinese restaurant. JIM takes
FAYE's arm.] Come right this way, please. [Points to bench]
You sit here. [She sits] Waiter be right with you. [JIM walks
around the bench three or four times.]

                    FAYE
Excuse me, I've been waiting a long time.

                          JIM
[Stopping]
Waiter give you menu?

                          FAYE
No.

                          JIM
I get him to bring you menu.

                          FAYE
The other waiter said . . .

                          JIM
Which waiter that, mam? [She points off to one side.] Oh,
that one? He go off work. He having dinner himself. [He
walks around the bench a couple of times.]

                          FAYE
I'm starved. Could we have some won ton soup?

                          JIM
[Stopping]
I'm not your waiter. I get you waiter. [He runs around the
bench once.   Then, pantomimes carrying a large covered
platter.] You in for big treat. When you order our specialty,
you in for big treat. [Pantomimes taking cover off platter.]
You don't look too happy. Whatsa matter? Pig have apple in
his mouth. You can't see his teeth.

                          FAYE
I haven't even seen a menu.

                          JIM
Oh, pig not for this table. Excuse me. [He walks around the
bench.]

                          FAYE
Please.

JIM

[Stopping]
Here is your bill. I hope you enjoy your meal.

FAYE

I haven't eaten.

JIM

Oh, you not like the meal? You not like Chinese food?

FAYE

Oh, I do.

JIM

You must be haole from the mainland. Not use to good
Chinese food.

FAYE

I haven't even seen a fortune cookie.

JIM

You not get a fortune cookie? Oh, I'm sorry. I get you one.
[He starts off again around the bench.]

FAYE

Come back.

JIM

[Comes around the bench and pantomimes holding a large box]
Here the fortune cookies you ordered. You going to have big
party? Nobody ever order 500 fortune cookies before. [He
stops acting and speaks to her in his normal voice.] Do you
remember that day?

FAYE

[Laughing]
Could I ever forget it! We went out and had a pizza, remember?

JIM

Mushroom and sausage and it was delicious!

FAYE
Remember the ride around Kaeina point? You were going to show me the island.

JIM
[With good humor]
You laughed at me then, didn't you?

FAYE
It is not everyday that one's hero gets stuck in the mud and has to be pulled out.

JIM
Remember? I said, 'Let me put some palm fronds under the back wheel.' Sit. [He motions for her to sit on one end of the bench as if it was the car. He goes to the other end of the bench and pantomimes putting the fronds under the wheel. They act out the incident.] Ready? When I say go, press on the accelerator. [To himself, stepping in imaginary mud] Damn mud up to my knees. Oh no. [She goes rnnn, rnnn, making the sound of a car starting, and he pantomimes trying to avoid a shower of mud from under the back wheels that is spraying him.] Stop! Stop! [She stops and looks out at him, wiping the mud from his eyes and face and body.]

FAYE
Didn't you say go? [They laugh together.]

JIM
We could go back to Hawaii.

FAYE
If all the flowers in the world looked alike, would they be beautiful?

JIM
I would bring you flowers every day.

FAYE
Would you?

                             JIM
Plumeria, orchid, frangipani. All the flowers I would lay at
your feet.

                             FAYE
Do you love me?

                             JIM
[Takes her hand]
Let's go back to Hawaii.

                             FAYE
Hawaii is gone. It's over.

                             JIM
No, it's not.

                             FAYE
It is. [She begins to cry.]

                             JIM
[Tenderly] Don't cry.
Don't cry.

                             FAYE
[Stopping]
I'm sorry. I know I said I wouldn't.

                             JIM
If you look at it logically, there's no reason why we couldn't
go back.

                             FAYE
[Pointing to the baby carriage]
There. That is the reason. Who would take care of her?

                             JIM
Faye, don't you think it's time we had a serious talk?

                         FAYE
If all the flowers in the world were blue, what color would the
ocean be?

                         JIM
No, Faye, don't! Let's talk!

                         FAYE
I'm not ready to talk.

                         JIM
You are ready, honey, you are.

                         FAYE
No, I'm not. Tell me of Hawaii.

                         JIM
Honey, baby, not now! Let's talk about the future.

                         FAYE
Tell me of Makaha. Tell me of Pats at Punalu.

                         JIM
No! I want to tell you of the future.

                         FAYE
[After a slight pause]
Answer me a question then?

                         JIM
All right.

                         FAYE
If all the flowers --

                         JIM
[Interrupting her, exasperated]
Oh God! I thought [walks away a few steps] . What difference
does it make.

                              FAYE
Jim, please understand.

                              JIM
[Turning and coming to her]
All right. I'll tell you what I understand. This has got to stop.
How long can we go on like this, Faye? How long? [Trying a
new approach] San Francisco? We could go there if you like.
Go down to Fisherman's Wharf and have some good seafood,
ride a cable car. We could do it, honey. Harry and Jackie
could meet us at the airport. We can drive in. Harry and Jackie will know a terrific Japanese restaurant.

                              FAYE
I don't think I want to see Harry and Jackie.

                              JIM
Well, all right, honey. We'll just call them. But, think! San
Francisco! Out to Sausalito! Come on.

                              FAYE
Out to Sausalito.

                              JIM
Wine tasting in the valley!

                              FAYE
Wine tasting in the valley!

                              JIM
The zoo!

                              FAYE
[Getting into the spirit of the repartee]
The zoo!

                              JIM
Top of the Mark!

                              FAYE
Top of the Mark!

                    JIM
Chinatown!

                    FAYE
Chinatown!

                    JIM
Palace of the Legion of Fine Arts!

                    FAYE
Palace of the Legion of Fine Arts!

                    JIM
[Begins to act out a scene again, this time a guide in the art gallery. FAYE plays the part of a visitor to the gallery.]
And so, if you will come this way, you can see a decided development in his artistic work that some critics say corresponds to
a similar development in his personal life.

                    FAYE
[Speaking to an imaginary person standing next to her, sotto
voce.]
His sex life!

                    JIM
[Hearing her.]
Madame! An artist's personal affairs are his personal affairs.
Now, if you will come this way.

                    FAYE
[A little louder than usual]
He must have had an active sex life.

                    JIM
Madame! An artist's sex life is of little concern.

                    FAYE
[Again, a little louder than usual]
It isn't to him.

                              JIM
[Stops acting and speaks in his normal voice.]
Remember how the group roared?

                              FAYE
And if I'm not mistaken, that little old lady pinched the man
in the green suit.

                              JIM
Yes.

                              FAYE
Jim, do you think we could have as much fun now in San Francisco as we did then?

                              JIM
More. It would be a second honeymoon.

                              FAYE
You think so?

                              JIM
I know so.

                              FAYE
[Pointing to the baby carriage]
Who would take care of her?

                              JIM
No one.

                              FAYE
No one? Who would take care of my Lela?

                              JIM
Honey, Lela is dead.

                              FAYE
Oh, no. That's just a rumor.

JIM
It's no rumor. She's dead.

FAYE
You don't love her or you wouldn't say that!

JIM
Faye, listen to me. Lela died a year ago. You know that.
She's with God now.

FAYE
No. My Lela's taking her nap.

JIM
She's not taking a nap!

FAYE
How can you be so cruel? When she wakes up, I'll show her all
the pretty flowers. Rock-a-bye baby on the tree top. [JIM
walks away. FAYE stares into space.]

JIM
[After a pause]
When was Lela born?

FAYE
You know that.

JIM
You tell me. I forgot.

FAYE
She was born two days before Christmas. She was our present
from Santa Claus.

JIM
How many years ago was that?

FAYE
It was the year mother had the candle holder made for our

FAYE [Cont'd.]

coffee table. She said it would light the baby's way into the world.

JIM

That's right. And how many years ago was that?

FAYE

It was . . .

JIM

It was four and a half years. Now tell me, Faye. If Lela was four and a half years old, would she still nap in a baby carriage?

FAYE

If all the flowers in the world had thorns, would people ever pick them?

JIM

Answer me! Would she?

FAYE

If all the flowers . . .

JIM

[Grabbing her by the shoulders and looking into her face] Answer me!! You know she couldn't be in the carriage! [She cries and he releases her and walks away. She stops crying after a moment or two.] I'm sorry, honey. Honest I am, but we've reached a time in our lives . . . oh God, why isn't life simple? Why can't we all just rest easy?

FAYE

What are you trying to tell me, Jim?

JIM

[After a pause]

Faye, one day when my old man was about 20 or 25, he looked at himself in the mirror and said, 'What the hell? I don't stand a chance in this world. Why should I get up off my duff.

                    JIM [Cont'd.]
The world isn't going to do a damn thing for me.' And so, my
father sat there with a can of beer in his hand until the day he
died and he never learned a thing. He never saw San Francisco,
never read a book, never ate Chinese food. All he ever cared
about was whether the Cubs were going to win the pennant.
And he wouldn't even get up out of that God damned chair to
go to the baseball stadium to see them play. We can't let that
happen to us. We've got to break that mirror, get up out of
that chair and go to the ball park, do you understand?

                    FAYE
I love you, Jim.

                    JIM
And I love you, Faye, but honey, I'm tired and I'm lonely. I
can't take the TV dinners, watching the tube by myself, the
silence is deafening. So, either this ends, or I'm going to walk
out of this flower garden forever. I will, believe me.

                    FAYE
There's another woman.

                    JIM
Don't be ridiculous.

                    FAYE
There is. Is she? . . .

                    JIM
Is she what?

                    FAYE
Is she?

                    JIM
Would it make any difference?

                    FAYE
No.

                    JIM
There is no other woman.

                    FAYE
Oh Jim, Jim, Jim.

                    JIM
Why not, Faye? Why not? Why not walk out of here with
me now?

                    FAYE
I have to take care of Lela.

                    JIM
Lela is dead!

                    FAYE
No. You're wrong, Jim. She's alive. In the morning, she
wakes up and calls for me. She has orange juice for breakfast,
and we talk and she dresses her dolls. It's true, Jim. [JIM
walks away.]

                    JIM
[After a pause]
Your mother phoned last night.

                    FAYE
Is she coming?

                    JIM
She said she'd try.

                    FAYE
How is she?

                    JIM
Said she gained five pounds.

                    FAYE
Oh, mother always says that. After all these years, she still

FAYE [Cont'd.]
wears a size eight dress. [JIM sits and looks into space.] Let
me ask you a question. Please. Come on.

JIM
All right.

FAYE
If the earth had two moons, what would happen to the tides?

JIM
They'd be twice as high, but half as frequent.

FAYE
[With exaggeration] You're kidding!

JIM
[With exaggeration while raising his hand in the scout salute]
Scouts honor! Faye, let's . . .

FAYE
[Interrupting him]
Why must you always come back to that? Why can't you
leave well enough alone?

JIM
Because it's there! It lives and it breathes. Let's go back to
Hawaii.

FAYE
To hell with Hawaii.

JIM
Faye!

FAYE
Hawaii is gone and finished. We can never go back.

JIM
Look, honey, we can. [Pause] Remember when we went to

JIM [Cont'd.]
Kauai and I asked that old Hawaiian how people in a paradise
like that knew that they loved one another? And he told me
they knew it when they were afraid together. Well, that's the
way it is with us, we have experienced something together,
only the two of us . . . oh God, I want to hold you so bad.
[She gets up and goes to the baby carriage.] Are you coming
with me or not? [She takes out of the carriage a large doll and
holds it close to her.]

FAYE
Lela.

JIM
[Going to her and taking the doll from her and showing it to
her.]
This is not Lela! This is a doll. You buy these things in stores,
you take them home to your children and they play with them.
This is not Lela. This is a doll. A doll.

FAYE
[Beginning to cry]
Oh God, can't you see, sometimes life becomes too much for
me.

JIM
[Walking away]
I'm sorry. [He has put the doll back in the carriage. FAYE
picks it up and takes it with her to the bench. She sits, holding
it but not paying attention to it and stares out into space.]

FAYE
The flowers are so pretty. If time would stop the pretty
flowers would never change. I wonder if I would tire of them?
[JIM sits next to her on the bench.]

JIM
[After a long pause]
Do you remember the kid's pool with the metal frame I had so
much trouble putting together?

                              FAYE
[With reference to the doll]
The pool Lela swims in?

                              JIM
Yes, that's it. The pool Lela swims in. It's still in the garage,
you know. [He stands] Let's put it together, okay? [He
holds his hand out to her, she takes it and rises.]

                              FAYE
Okay. [They begin to act out the following sequence, and
pantomime all the actions as they speak. The pool is one
which has a metal frame a foot and a half in width and about
fifteen to twenty feet in length. The ends are attached and
the metal forms a circle. A large plastic sheet is put in the
center and is held to the top of the metal frame by a plastic
cap fifteen to twenty feet in length and an inch in width that
fits over the plastic sheet and the top of the frame. The bar-
becue he pantomimes is a hibachi.]

                              JIM
You get the plastic while I attach this.

                              FAYE
[In reference to the plastic sheet she is carrying]
Heavy.

                              JIM
This damn thing! You need a PhD in engineering to put it together. Got it! Now, let's attach the plastic.

                              FAYE
There we go.

                              JIM
[Pointing to one side]
Turn the water on.

                              FAYE
[She does so.]

FAYE [Cont'd.]

Is it filling?

JIM

[Holding the hose into the pool]
Yes.

FAYE

Lela loves this pool.

JIM

Maybe she'd like to swim in it, or at least splash around.

FAYE

Maybe she would.

JIM

Why don't you get her?

FAYE

Really?

JIM

Really. Why don't you get her and sit there by the pool with
her while I go fix us some iced tea. [He goes to one side and
she goes and gets the doll.]

FAYE

Come on, baby. Daddy's fixed the pool so we can go for a
swim. No, the water's not cold. It's warm. [Puts the doll in
the center of the pool.] There. Isn't that nice. Look, here's
your beach ball. Oh, you want Mommy to blow it up more?
[She does so.] Here we are. Throw it to Mommy. That's it.
That's it.

JIM

Here's your tea. [He pantomimes pouring a glass of tea and
handing one to her, then pouring one for himself.] Don't
splash Daddy, Lela.

                              FAYE
Throw Daddy the ball.

                              JIM
Atta girl. [To FAYE] We barbecued that day, didn't we,
honey?

                              FAYE
[After a slight hesitation]
Yes.

                              JIM
Then, I had better get the fire started. [As he prepares the
barbecue] Remember, we talked about how we used to bar-
becue in Hawaii all the time?

                              FAYE
Yes, and I said it would be nice to have teriyaki again.

                              JIM
When I lit the fire, remember what I said to Lela?

                              FAYE
You said . . .

                              JIM
I said, watch the big flames. Ready? [Pantomimes the fire
going up] Poof! And then, Lela got out of the pool to get the
ball. Take Lela out of the pool, honey, to get the ball. Go
ahead. [She does so.]

                              FAYE
All right.

                              JIM
Then, what happened?

                              FAYE
Lela got out and went around the side of the house.

                    JIM
Did you say anything to her?

                    FAYE
Yes. I said, don't go in the road.

                    JIM
Tell it to her, honey.

                    FAYE
[Holding the doll]
Don't go in the road, Lela baby.

                    JIM
And what did she say?

                    FAYE
She said, 'I won't, Mommy.'

                    JIM
That's right. And then what happened?

                    FAYE
I went back and took another sip of my tea.

                    JIM
Go ahead. [She goes to the bench and pantomimes taking a
sip from her glass.] And then?

                    FAYE
And then . . .

                    JIM
Go on, Faye, talk to me and show me what you did that day.

                    FAYE
I took a sip of tea. And the coals were ready on the fire, and
I said I'll get the meat, and I went inside and I came back out
and I gave the teriyaki to you and you put it on the fire and
then I sat down [She sits]. I was tired.

                              JIM
[Lifting her up]
No, you didn't sit down. What did you do, Faye honey? Do
you remember?

                              FAYE
I . . . I . . .

                              JIM
You walked around the house to see where Lela was. Didn't
you honey?

                              FAYE
Yes, that's it.

                              JIM
Go ahead, honey, walk around the side of the house where
Lela is. [She walks to one side.]

                              FAYE
I said, Lela do you want to come back and swim awhile before dinner? And she said, no, Mommy, I'll stay here. I'm
showing the beach ball to my doll Mary Elizabeth. She likes
it. I said, that's fine. I'll call you when dinner is ready and
then I came back and I had another drink of my tea and I went
and got the salad and you said . . . you said . . .

                              JIM
What kind of dressing?

                              FAYE
And I said, French from the blender and I came outside and I
put the salad down and I got the silverware and placemats for
the redwood table and I took a drink and I got napkins and
then, and then, and then . . .

                              JIM
Then what?

                              FAYE

I heard a sound.

                              JIM

What sound? What was the sound, Faye?

                              FAYE

It was loud and grating.

                              JIM

And then?

                              FAYE

And then, we heard nothing and we ran and . . .

                              JIM

And what happened??

                              FAYE

[In tears]
No! No! Oh God, no! [She breaks down and after a few
moments at the point when she is sobbing softly, JIM speaks.]

                              JIM

[Picking up the doll and putting it on the bench]
We picked up our Lela and put her on the table and she didn't
say anything.

                              FAYE

She wasn't in the road, Jim, she wasn't even in the road.

                              JIM

[Tenderly]
Faye.

                              FAYE

Jim, why us? Of all the people in the world, why us?

                              JIM

I don't know. [Walks away a few steps thinking and after a

JIM [Cont'd.]
pause, speaks.] I heard a story once about a man who had a
dream in the middle of the night. He dreamt he saw a vision, a
fire burning, and he asked the vision, why? Why do I live and
children die? And a voice from the fire said, 'Endure not to
know.'

FAYE

That's no answer.

JIM

No, I don't suppose it is.

FAYE

Where does that leave us now, Jim?

JIM

It leaves us free to go home.

FAYE

And what then? [Said simply] Lela. Lela. Lela.

JIM

[Going to her with intensity]
Honey, honey. It's time to face up to the fact that our Lela is
dead and has been for a year, and that you have a husband who
is alive and breathing and who needs you and wants to take
you away from this flower garden and all the memories of Lela
and start making some new memories.

FAYE

Lela likes teriyaki.

JIM

Faye, honey, please, don't start that again.

FAYE

Funny how she likes teriyaki almost more than any other kind
of meat. Why does she like it so?

                                    JIM
Faye, please!

                                    FAYE
Teriyaki and Kool-aid. She likes orange Kool-aid with teriyaki.
I'll fix her some.

                                    JIM
No, Faye, no! Stop it! Stop it!

                                    FAYE
[Pantomiming the action as she speaks]
You just open the package like this and pour it into the pitcher. We empty the package in the big pitcher and pour in
water and add sugar. Maybe Daddy would like some. Give it
to Daddy.

                                    JIM
[Spoken at the same time she speaks the above lines]
Faye, honey, stop! Stop it. I love you. We have something
special. Stop it, please, oh God, stop it.

          [A NURSE in a white uniform enters and points
          to the watch on her wrist indicating that time is
          up and it is time to leave. JIM rises, after looking
          at the NURSE, and nods his head. He starts to
          walk away. FAYE, in the meantime, has continued
          her speech.]

                                    FAYE
Where is Daddy going? Lela, Daddy is going to work. Say bye-
bye to Daddy.

          [The NURSE exits, along with JIM, who doesn't look
          back.]

Lela, look at the pretty flowers. Lela, if all the flowers in the
world could speak, what do you think they'd say?

                              CURTAIN